Wished Away

Wished Away

Jonathan Lee

BOLD PUBLISHING

Cover photograph by urikyo33 via
Pixabay

ISBN: 979-8-98-843920-2

Bold Publishing is a small
independent publishing imprint.
Your support is greatly appreciated.

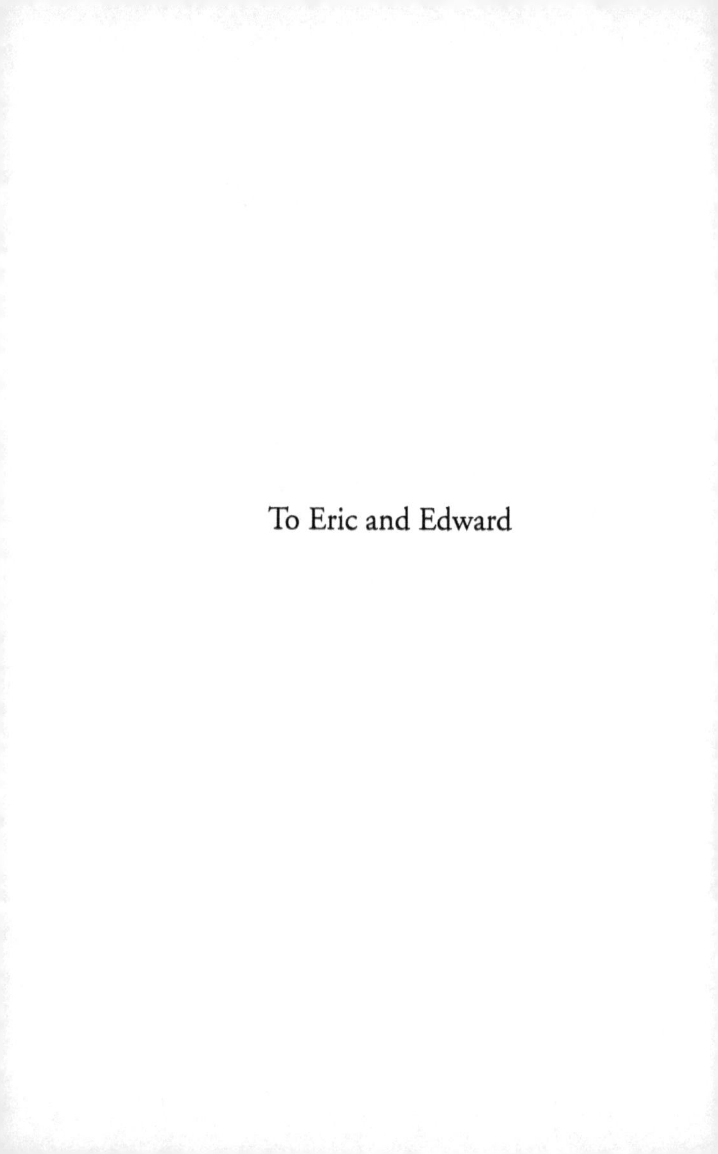

To Eric and Edward

I

FOG rolled across the freeway, beneath the starless sky of an autumn night mircd in mclancholy. The strange orange glow of street lamps bathed his surroundings in an unseemly warmth for such a cold night, mocking his sadness and hinting of golden days now seeming so far behind. A low fence, half his height at most, was all that separated him from the mad rush of semi trucks barreling down the road like trackless trains.

He felt like maybe taking off his shoes. That's what people did in this kind of situation, didn't they? Of course, that was usually with jumping. A long fall from some dizzying height. Here, there wouldn't be a drop of any kind. Just a steady walk into a rushing river. A river of traffic that would sweep him violently off his feet. Maybe it would feel nice to feel grass beneath those feet one more time before he leapt to his end.

With a gulp and a shake of his head, he turned from the fence and looked back. The battered parking lot of a cheap motel beyond the cold muck of grass and mud before him. Even this dismal sight had a strange beauty. That same strange mocking beauty of golden lamp lights glowing in the fog. He didn't really want it to end. What did he really want?

Attention. Some acknowledgment of his pain. A smidgen of validation. Some grand gesture to show the world he was suffering. But what was the point of such a show if he never got to take his bow? He would never see the applause after the final curtain. The performance would simply be cut short out on the road. A grisly mess for befuddled strangers.

Was it so wrong to want to be acknowledged? To be comforted? Perhaps even to be loved?

His chest started to convulse with something like quiet laughter. But it wasn't laughter. There's a curiously fine line between laughter and weeping. The torso trimmers. The mouth gasps.

Tears may start to roll down the cheeks. But after a moment or two of observation, it becomes clear whether a person is filled with mirth or melancholy.

His aching heart was filled with the latter. But there was another strange correlation between his pitiful sobbing state and merriment. He felt like a child again. A scared lost child.

When Thomas was eight years old, his older brother refused to play with him one night. Alone and distraught, the game pad trembling in his little hands, he started to cry. He whimpered and sobbed as he hit the sides of his head with his palms. And then in a fit of anger and shame that he didn't fully understand he grabbed a nearby baseball bat, and crawled under his brother's bed. There he shoved the bat into his abdomen again and again.

"I wanna kill myself!" he shouted when his brother asked him what he was doing.

After a moment of quiet gasping tears, the subtle sound of swishing fabric and creaking floorboards came from behind. It was his brother crawling under the bed with him. Harold didn't quite fit as well as Thomas, and so Harry pulled his little brother to the edge, and there on the floor, curled up behind, he held him.

"Tom, I'm… sorry," his brother whispered. The rhythm of little Tom's weeping slowed and then ended with a final sigh, as he rested there safe and secure in his brother's arms. Arms like a father. Like the father he never knew.

Their own father had died five years earlier.

Back in the present, the middle-aged Thomas Wilson was alone. So utterly alone. His heart was in greater shambles than the beat up old asphalt of that cold empty parking lot. It had been ripped out of his chest, thrown to the ground, and trampled.

"I know we had an agreement," she said with an infuriating calm.

"An agreement?! We had a *marriage!*"

He had shouted. He had screamed. He had writhed in agony. And she, in turn, was quiet. Sorrowful, but not sorry. She made no defense. And, in time… she left. That was the end of it. The end of the world. The end of everything he thought he knew.

So now here he was, alone in a cold lonely space filled with fog and despair. The night before his birthday, on the day just after Thanksgiving. She had never gotten along with his family. And so at the last minute she had booked this cheap little motel in the middle of nowhere.

According to the address it was in Perrysburg, but that was some kind of cartographic joke. In reality it was really outside any of the tiny towns and villages that littered northern Ohio. A little beggarly building nestled between a truck stop and a tire repair outfit. Crowded by cars and heavy machinery on both ends, but nary a human being in sight.

Looking out on that landscape of machinery in the dim dark soup of his surroundings, he reflected on his own murky life. Wandering, directionless, he had stumbled into network engineering. Surrounded more by machines than men. He met his own wife online… for whatever worth that was now.

"Such a waste…" he muttered to himself and sniffed. He reached under his shirt and pulled out a pendant. A bit of custom jewelry his late father had made. As he fondled it near his chest, his heart ached for simplicity. A time when there weren't so many *connections* in the world, coiled up like a nest of snakes. A time like before he was born.

As he gathered himself together to make his way back to his empty motel room, the clouds above parted a little.

Wished Away

A patch of starry sky appeared in the distance, and inside that little heavenly window a stripe of light streaked across. A shooting star.

"Heh…" he sniffed and then thought for a moment before whispering to himself, "I wish tomorrow was a day before the web."

The world wide web, he meant. That tangled mess of media online which complicated so many lives. It was like Pandora's proverbial box, a mythic mess of troubles unleashed on the world by CERN a matter of months before he was born.

It was late and he longed now for sleep. And so he stumbled into bed, fully clothed. In the dark he quickly drifted into a sad slumber, his one comforting thought that he had wished the world away.

Wished Away

Jonathan Lee

II

THE next morning Tom awoke in that groggy fog of forgetfulness that makes a man feel out of place with his surroundings. *The motel room. Right.* Yet, even as he assured himself of where he was, that feeling of disorientation lingered. Something was… different. Something about the color of the walls or the ambient sound. He couldn't quite place it.

A chunky click snapped his attention to an old bedside alarm clock to his right. "Heh…" he snorted with amusement at the sight of that curiously retro flip clock. He had forgotten how cheap this motel was. But then… how cheap were flip clocks anymore? A little LED clock would probably be cheaper, really. An old flip clock would actually be something of a collector's item at this point, wouldn't it?

He shook the thought away and rubbed his eyes, before rising to his feet, taking a nice long stretch, and having a look around. His suitcase was gone, along with his laptop and everything else.

"Figures…" he muttered to himself. Clearly she had cleaned out the room.

In fact, as he regarded the room in more detail, *cleaned* was the operative word indeed. The waste basket was empty. The smattering of receipts intermixed with last night's lo mein was gone. Apart from a mild impression where he had slept, the bed sheets were neatly made. The entire room was spotless.

"Huh…" he grunted and scratched the back of his head. But in the end he shrugged and made his way to the door. According to the old flip clock it was almost 9 AM, so it was probably best to check out by now. The sooner he could get out of the sticks the better. He wasn't sure where he'd go from here and she probably took the car, but he'd cross that bridge when there was a bridge to cross—out here everything was too plain and flat for bridges.

Wished Away

Jonathan Lee

III

AS he made his way around the shabby little wing of the motel, the bright light of a strangely warm morning forced him to squint as he stammered his way toward the front office. He was only a few yards from the quaint columns of the motel's covered driveway when his eyes finally adjusted enough to see with some measure of comfort. And it was there that he stopped and turned to note the newly paved parking lot he had just traversed.

With another furrowed brow, he scratched the back of his head, and shook the feeling away before proceeding. Or at least he tried. As Tom entered the front office, that strange sense of disorientation washed over him like the crestless wave of a sea swell. He hadn't particularly paid attention to the office when he checked in, and thus it was difficult to pinpoint how precisely, but he was increasingly aware that somehow things were very… *different.*

"Hi! Welcome to the Simply 7! How can I help you?" said a bubbly woman behind the counter.

"Heh, hi. Yeah, I just wanted to check out actually."

"Oh! Yes, certainly. Your name, sir?"

"Thomas Wilson."

The chipper woman nodded and proceeded clicking and clacking away on a keyboard. A little old wall-mounted CRT television blared in the corner of the room. *"Al, why haven't I leaped yet?" All new episode, this Wednesday…*

"Hmm," the woman said with a furrowed brow, "I can't seem to find you in here…"

"Oh?"

"Hold on, it might just be me. I'm not used to this new system and all. Let me just check the register." With that she pulled out a three ring binder and flipped through a few pages. "Did you perhaps check in under a different name?"

"Huh? No, I don't… maybe Amber? Amber Wilson?"

After a brief moment of checking she replied, "No… not seeing that name either."

"Heh, does that mean my stay is free?"

The woman chuckled nervously. "Uh, do you recall what room you were staying in?"

"Uh, not sure, actually…" he began, "Here. Can you read what you need from my key card?"

"I *think* so. Let me check…" She took the magstripe card from his hand and slid it through a reader on the desk. After a moment she tried swiping it again, and then again, each time her brow getting a little more rumpled with concern and confusion. Finally, she turned the card over and examined the image on the back.

"Sir… are you sure you're at the right location?"

"What? What do you—I woke up here." He snorted and smirked incredulously.

"Well, it's just… this card… it—it says Simply 7. But the logo is different. See?" She held up another card for comparison. "And I'm not able to read this one."

His eyes widened as he examined the cards side by side in her hands. A few blinks and a gulp. His heart started to pound. "I don't—I don't… What?"

He spun his head around to the window behind him and looked out on that parking lot with its new smooth asphalt. He thought back to his room. The differences. Had he been drugged? Abducted? For what? Just to steal his laptop or his clothes? He frantically patted his pockets. "Keys, wallet, phone. Never leave home…" he muttered the sing-song chant he used to remind himself. He gave one last tap to his chest, and felt the pendant there. Finding everything in its place, he breathed out a sigh.

"So, uh… is there anything else?" the woman asked.

"I guess… not… heh."

Peering out the window, he came back to his moment of need. She took the car. He was going to need a ride. He pulled out his phone. No bars. Figures. He was in the sticks and all. No networks listed in the WiFi network list.

"Actually," he said turning around, "can I still get on your WiFi? Not seeing it listed."

"Why what?"

"The WiFi. Y'know, internet?"

"Internet…? Oh! I think I've heard of that."

"Heh… you're—are you… joking?"

"What?" she asked with a nervous chuckle.

He looked away from the woman and panned over the room. The little old CRT television in the corner. The CRT monitor at the lobby desk. A simple push button phone on a hook. And that's when he spotted the newspaper. His heart raced as he read the date, confirming a growing suspicion. But it couldn't be. Was he dreaming? Some elaborate joke? Amber? No. No, she just wanted to go. Was there a simpler explanation?

"How long have you had this?" he asked, his voice ever so slightly shaking as he tried to keep his cool.

"Just came this morning I think, why?"

"So this, uh… you're telling me this is today's date?"

"Yes—wait, no, sorry. I forgot. That's from yesterday. Today's the 29th."

"Of April…"

"Yep."

"1993…" he said with a gulp.

She nodded casually.

"Th-thanks…" he said, and wandered thoughtlessly toward the door.

"Sir?"

"Huh?"

She glanced toward his hand. "The paper?"

"Oh, right… sorry…" He slid the paper back on the desk and meandered back out the door.

"Have a nice day!"

He didn't acknowledge her farewell. He couldn't. He was struggling just to stay upright. And so he ambled along outside, noting with a gulp a number of disturbing differences from last night. The tire repair shop was nowhere to be seen now. All the vehicles were notably of an older design. The nearby highway even sounded quieter.

IV

HE finally found himself wandering the snack aisles of the truck stop a couple blocks south. Perhaps if he ate something, he might clear his head. And so at last, he shuffled up to the counter in a bit of a daze, holding a glass bottle of some strawberry kiwi concoction and a bag of cheap donuts.

"Breakfast of champions, eh?" the man behind the counter said with a smirk.

"Huh? Oh… heh… yeah…"

Two men stood behind him in line. "Did you hear about the outcome of the King follow up trial?"

"King?" the other man asked.

"Yeah, Rodney King. They tried the cops again. The Feds this time. Couple weeks back."

"No, what happened?"

"Goddamn jury found 'em guilty. Violating 'civil rights.' Such a joke."

"Pfft, figures…"

"Maybe *we* should riot this time."

The cashier tapped away at the register while the men were talking. He looked up at Tom once he finished. "That'll be two fifty."

Tom instinctively pulled out his debit card from his wallet, but then hesitated before handing it to the cashier. Would it work? If this surreal scenario he was in was really real, it wouldn't, would it? He didn't have an account with the bank in 1993. He wasn't even born until November.

"Sorry," the cashier said, interrupting Tom's train of thought. "Cash only. We actually do have a card reader, but it's down right now."

Tom put his card back and peered into the long neglected cash pocket, and discovered two single dollar bills. He slowly retrieved them with a gulp. Possibly the only cash he had to his name at this point.

"I… I guess I'll just get the donuts then…"

"Alright," the cashier said as he quickly tapped away on the register. "That'll be one twenty three."

"How much is your water? I didn't see—"

"Water?" the cashier asked with a snicker. "That's still free, champ. Water fountain's by the restrooms. There."

Tom turned and looked toward the restroom doors in the distance, confused. Right. Water fountains. When he turned back, the cashier counted back seventy-seven cents in change. Three quarters and a couple pennies. 1990, 1990, 1993, 1991, 1989. The 1993 one was a quarter. An especially shiny quarter. Brand new. He marveled as he turned it over in his hand.

Seventy-seven cents. Some donuts. Keys, wallet, phone. The clothes on his back. The pendant and its necklace. This was the meager sum of his possessions now. He couldn't even pawn his wedding ring. He had thrown it at Amber the night before. He could pawn the pendant, but… no. He couldn't do that. It probably wouldn't fetch much anyways.

"You okay, buddy?" a deep but kind voice asked with concern.

He looked up to see warm eyes beneath two furrowed brows. A clean-shaven face, with that vaguely gray wash of subtle stubble seen on men with quick-growing beards. Flannel shirt and blue jeans. Plastic bag of something in his left hand.

"I—I'm not sure," Tom finally replied. And then he peered back down at his change. With another gulp, he slowly slipped it into his pants pocket.

While Tom stared at the floor and sighed, the kind stranger quietly bit his lower lip in contemplation and darted his eyes around for a moment. Finally the man spoke. "I don't mean to pry, but are you maybe… down on your luck? If you want, I could get you something."

Tom snapped his eyes to the stranger, and thought for a moment himself. He darted his eyes around from the stranger to the door and back. He then suddenly blurted it out. "I could use a ride."

"Oh…" the stranger remarked, taken a little aback. "Um…"

Tom stared at him with a gaze of unintentionally pleading eyes. He then broke his gaze and shook his head. "I mean… I don't know…"

"Sure."

"Really?"

"Yeah, yeah. Yeah, I can do that."

"T-thank you. Yeah, I definitely— I'll definitely need one."

"Alright, well… uh, this way then…" The man led the way outside, and Tom followed sheepishly as the tall stranger marched along toward a row of semi-trucks behind the storefront of the truck stop. Tom now started to wonder what he was getting himself into. He was planning on getting in the car with a stranger before. But somehow the comfort of some vague accountability that came with a rating system would have given him assurance. Was that just some false sense of security? Perhaps the superior sense of assurance was seeing kindness in a man's eyes.

"Where ya headed?"

"Oh, uh… Perrysburg?"

"Ah, you're not very far out then, eh?"

"Yeah, heh…"

"The name's Sam, by the way."

"Tom," he replied as he grasped Sam's extended hand and exchanged a shake along with an awkward smile.

"It's a bit of a climb," Sam remarked as he opened the passenger side door of the truck's cabin. Two steps before the base of the cabin. He had never been in a semi until this very moment. For some reason the thought filled him with a strange sense of amusement. How many other simple common things had he never experienced? Now that he was on the threshold of the cabin, he wondered at the fact that he never really had noticed how large these things really were.

And now he was about to climb into one. Was this the right choice? What other choice did he have? He could walk. It would take a few hours, but he could do it. Who knows what peril might be out there on the road? Every step in life is a calculated risk. And here he was about to take the final step into the cabin.

"You, uh… ready?" Sam asked, a little nervous himself. Tom peered at that kind face. A strangely familiar face. Was that why it seemed he could trust him?

"Yeah… yeah, I'm ready."

V

WIDE expanses of flat farm-land stretched out from both sides of the highway, interrupted by an occasional smattering of trees. Gentle clouds rolled by as they strolled along the road. The high cab of the truck made their pace seem almost leisurely. The peaceful lazy landscape distracted Tom from his worries for a moment, as they rode along in relative quiet.

"So, are you from Perrysburg then?" Sam asked, breaking the silence.

"What? Oh, uh… no, not really. My mother lives there. I was—I was actually born in Maumee."

"Oh yeah? No kidding? I live between Maumee and Holland myself."

"It's, uh, a lovely part of town to be sure—Maumee, that is."

"It definitely beats other parts of Toledo. I'm not in the nicest part of Maumee, but I still wanted to pay extra for a nice apartment. Eventually I'd like to buy a house. Probably not in Perrysburg anytime soon, but something not far from there."

Tom nodded and let out a little nervous cough. An awkward silence sat between them for another moment.

"Got any kids?"

"Me? Uh… no, no, not yet."

"So you want kids?"

"Uh, yes, yeah, I would like kids… some day…" With that Tom gazed off into the distance wistfully and let out a quiet sigh.

"That's why I got the place I did. It's a bit of a stretch, but my wife and I agreed it was worth it. My son starts Kindergarten next year and there's this Catholic school that's supposed to be really good. I'm not Catholic myself, but it's supposed to be a really good school. Really—really good."

Tom nodded quietly. His attention was torn between his traveling companion and the increasingly beautiful surroundings. Trees steadily replaced the flat farms, and occasional outlying houses popped up between them. Between the growing wistful blanket of clouds and the cottage like homes dotting the countryside, the surroundings were starting to look like some bucolic work of Thomas Kinkade or Norman Rockwell. Baseball and apple pie. Families gathered around giant turkeys.

But that's when he remembered there would be no turkey dinner out there. It wasn't November. Not anymore. It was April. And it wasn't some forgotten American past that never really was. It was... *the 90's.* He rubbed his eyes at the thought. Was this all really real?

"So, uh, what do you do?" Sam asked.

"Huh?"

"I mean—for a living… normally, that is," Sam tried to clarify, and gave a nervous little cough.

"Oh, uh… I'm a network engineer, actually."

"*Network* Engineer?"

"Yeah, as in… uh… computer systems."

"Wow! Like, uh, what was that… ethernet? You work with ethernet? Or token ring?"

"Uh… heh, yeah. Ethernet. Although most of my time these days is spent tweaking configuration scripts for routers. Token ring is pretty depre… cated…" Tom trailed off. He had momentarily forgotten his peculiar situation and then recalled it all at once. A wry smirk that came to his face with the mention of "token ring" had slowly faded when he got to the point of explaining its largely out-moded usage. In 1993 that wasn't quite as much the case.

"That's really cool, man. I'm trying to get into computers myself. Really the wave of the future, eh?"

Tom peered at Sam, noting the ex-cited grin and spark of intelligence in his eyes. He couldn't recall meeting too many truck drivers, if any, but some-how Sam didn't seem to match the profile he had in his mind. He took it as a rebuke of his own prejudice.

"Heh… I don't meet too many people familiar with network topolo-

gies. Let alone anyone, uh… express-
ing enthusiasm for it."

"Yeah, yeah I bet…" Sam re-
marked, and then seeming to sense
Tom's own thoughts, continued "and
I'm sure especially not too many truck
drivers, eh?"

Tom laughed. "Well… I have to
admit I'm not sure I've met too many
truck drivers to be honest."

"To be honest myself, I don't really
feel I fit in with my fellow drivers. I
guess it's a good thing I work mostly
alone."

Tom nodded and turned his attention back to the road. He figured now
might be a good time to compare
routes. Instinctively he pulled out his
phone to check the map, but quietly
muttered a rebuke of his own reflexive

forgetfulness, and let out a frustrated sigh.

"I've only been doing this for less than a year," Sam spoke up again. "I actually just came out of the Navy."

"Oh yeah?" Tom asked. "My father was in the Navy."

"Really? Do you know which service or fleet?"

"I'm… not really sure, sorry. I never really got a chance to know my father to be honest."

"Oh… I'm sorry."

"It's okay, umm… I think he was, uh, on a submarine."

"Really?" Sam asked with some excitement. "I was in the silent service myself. Earned my dolphins back in '89. I actually ended up serving in the

Iraq war. A lot of people don't know how critical submarines were in—"

"Oh hey!" Tom interjected. "Did we just pass I-75?"

"Oh, uh, yeah. Did we need to turn there?"

"It's okay. If maybe you just turn left on, uh, Sandusky we can get back on the 75. My mother's house is… or was…" Tom trailed off with a sigh. This exercise was seeming more futile. What was he hoping to accomplish going back? She wouldn't be there. Would she? He had to be sure. Was he really back in 1993? If his surreal situation was really real, he wasn't sure where his mother was living precisely back then. Or, that is… *now?*

"Sandusky. Sure thing."

A few minutes passed before the highway quickly narrowed to a neighborhood avenue, after a gradual bend near an old colonial style congregational church. The semi felt increasingly out of place on the increasingly cramped quiet street of the small town.

"You have any issues driving in town like this?"

"Nah, I'm not hauling anything hazardous anyhow."

"What *are* you hauling?"

"I tend to haul a lot of glass goods. This time it's light bulbs."

"That's not considered hazardous?"

"No. Why would they be?"

"Well, fluorescent bulbs contain mercury and all."

"No, no. Nothing like that. This is just the cheap ones like you find in your house."

"Like old incand—uh, right… right…"

"Alright, here's Sandusky. Where are we going from here?"

"You know what? Maybe, uh, actually if it's okay it's—it's quicker to stay on this road and turn left on Fort Meigs."

"You sure?"

"I, uh, I think so… yeah…"

Tom sighed again as he looked down to his phone. A useless brick at this point. He was used to driving to his mom's by memory, taking exit 2 from the 75. At least he thought it was the 2. He mostly just exited when he saw the Salesco coming up. Would the Salesco even be there?

Wished Away

Jonathan Lee

VI

FTER navigating the quiet by-
ways and tranquil traffic of the
small town, they finally arrived
at his mother's house. It actually
looked much the same as he was expecting, barring a number of signifi-
cant details. For one, the Christmas
decorations were absent. The tacky little reindeer his mother insisted she

loved were nowhere to be seen. Neither were the string of lights and snowflakes she always put out shortly after Halloween. But most disconcerting of all was the hanging "For sale" sign at the edge of the bare lawn.

"Is this it?" Sam asked with a hint of concern.

"Yes," Tom said, "but then… no." Sam waited quietly, while Tom peered out the window and sighed. Finally he spoke again. "I guess, now, I don't really have anywhere to go."

It was the right address. The number was right. The neighbor's pink flamingo was there. He kept it around year long. On the other side, the beat up old lawnmower was there in the other neighbor's yard. It was definitely the right place. Just the wrong time.

Wished Away

"Say… you hungry?"

◇

Tom found himself following Sam into a "Marty's" a couple miles away, on the other side of the interstate. Sam had insisted that donuts weren't a proper meal, and the morning was growing later. And so he took Tom out for brunch.

"Thank you for this. I really appreciate it."

"Hey, you're more than welcome. We live in the land of plenty." Tom nodded and smiled in return, and Sam continued as he gazed out the window of the diner, "I've had rough times myself. And I ask myself 'What if it were one of my sons?' Y'know?"

Tom, stared down at the table and nodded somberly. Since he was around ten years old, he longed for a son. Growing up with an older brother, he wondered now and again what it would be like to have a younger brother of his own. And at some point it occurred to him that this was perhaps what it might be like to have a son. And that thought grew into a quiet desire for children in general.

"My wife. She never really wanted children."

"Really?" Sam asked incredulously.

"Yeah," Tom replied mournfully. "I guess that's part of why it never really worked out."

Sam studied Tom in silence, as Tom continued to gaze at—and really through—the table. Sad peering eyes lost in a past that was strangely yet future.

"Can I get you anything else?" a heavyset middle-aged woman asked as she refilled their drinks.

"Heh, a job I guess..." Tom muttered under his breath.

"What's that, sweetie?"

"Uh nothing, nothing."

"I think we're good, thanks," Sam said with a polite smile.

Another moment passed after the waitress left, before Sam finally spoke. "My first marriage was a mess." Tom looked up from the table inquisitively. Sam in turn was gazing out the window now. "We were not made for each other. Or if we were, it was a match made in Hell, heh..."

Sam returned his gaze to Tom and continued, "Some people say that not every relationship's meant to be. Personally, I think *every* relationship can be meaningful. It just might not mean what we think it means. You think you've met the love of your life, but that person might just be the prelude to a grander story. Not everyone we meet is who we think they are."

Tom nodded quietly and looked back to the table. His mind chewed on Sam's strangely sage words. It was a kind of meal he wasn't expecting in this roadside diner.

"It's a bit of a cliché and all," Sam said, "but I guess the point is… be careful what you wish for. You might just get it."

"What you wish for…" Tom repeated slowly and then gasped.

"What is it?"

"The shooting star. I completely forgot." Tom darted his eyes to and fro.

"Shooting star?"

"Yes. That's it. I can't believe it."

"Believe what?"

Tom's wide darting eyes relaxed and fixed on Sam. He blinked a bit, looked away, and sighed. "You wouldn't believe me."

"Heh, I try to be pretty open-minded," Sam replied.

"I can hardly believe it myself."

"I'm listening."

"What's today date?"

"The 29th," Sam replied.

Tom gestured for him to go on.

"Of April."

Tom gestured again, rolling his hands.

"1993. April 29th, 1993. Why?"

"Right. Well, for me… yesterday was November 24th, 2023. Today was supposed to be my 30th birthday, and instead now I wasn't even born until November 25th of this year—1993."

"Heh," Sam chuckled. "You—you're joking, right?"

"I told you you wouldn't believe me."

Sam chuckled some more, cocked his head, narrowed his eyes, and peered at Tom incredulously. "So, you—you're really telling me you think you're from the future."

"From your perspective. This is all the past for me."

"Right, sure, yeah," Sam replied and chuckled some more, before stopping with a nervous cough. When he could see that Tom was completely serious, he started to grow concerned.

"Look. Here," Tom directed as he pulled out his wallet. "What do you make of this?" He pointed at the birth date on his driver's license.

Sam relaxed a bit. It was now less likely that Tom was mentally disturbed. His current conjecture became that this was some kind of practical joke. "Oh, haha, good one. Really fancy." Tom turned it over in his hands. "Is that a hologram? Wow, how much did you spend to make this thing?"

Tom sighed. Of course Sam would think it all an elaborate hoax. He would think the same thing were he in Sam's shoes. In fact, at first he essentially did. And his mind was called back to earlier at the hotel. Under his breath he muttered to himself "keys, wallet, phone…"

Phone. That last word reminded him. Of course! Sam was tech-savvy. Maybe…

"Okay, okay, take a look at this," Tom said as he pulled out his phone.

"A look at what?"

Tom looked at the screen. All black. The button on the side wasn't responding.

"Shit," Tom said. The phone was dead.

"Eh?"

"Wait, wait wait…" Tom said as he frantically padded himself. With a sigh of relief he pulled out a cord from his jacket pocket and plugged it into his phone.

He then pulled out the rest of the cord. And with that, his panic returned. USB-C.

"What kind of cord is that?"

"Fuck! No, no no."

Sam was starting to get concerned again. Tom patted himself down and gave another relieved sigh. And with that he pulled out a little white box with a couple protruding metal prongs. The AC adapter.

"Okay, I just need to plug this in. And then you'll see something like nothing you've really seen before."

"Heh, alright."

Once the phone was plugged in, Sam stared at the charging animation.

"Huh, color screen? Is that some kind of new gameboy?"

"Ha, no. This is essentially an entire personal computer system in your pocket."

"A pocket PC?"

"Yep. Microsoft even called it that, and that wasn't even a phone. That was something like twenty years ago."

"Phone?"

"Yeah, smart phone. It's like a PDA and cell phone in one."

"Oh, I know about cell phones. I'm planning on getting one soon actually."

"Okay, here here, check this out," Tom said with some excitement, as he powered on his phone and pointed at the boot screen.

"Goggle? Are you saying these are goggles now too? Heh."

"No, Google. This is an Android phone."

"So it's a robot now, eh?"

Tom rolled his eyes. "Just watch."

Sam's wry smirk faded away as he watched the boot animation complete and Tom started to demonstrate the device's features. He watched as Tom showed him how the touchscreen responded. His eyes widened as high definition graphical interfaces came and went with dynamic real-time rendered animations. His jaw went slack as Tom showed off the built-in camera. His smirking incredulity had transformed into shock, a bit of confusion, and a growing sense of awe.

"Th—this… is… amazing!"

"In my time, it's common place. Mundane even."

Sam blinked and shook his head, as though awakening from a spell. "Okay, okay, but wait… as incredible as this thing is… Time travel? That's even more incredible. Extraordinary claims require extraordinary evidence. How do I know you're not, uh—I don't know—escaping from the government with some top secret advanced technology or something?"

"Heh, sounds like The X-Files."

"The what?"

"Oh, that's not out yet?"

Sam simply stared in confusion.

Tom continued, "I have to applaud your imagination, and your epistemology is sound. It's a fair point, heh." There certainly was more to this curious trucker than he ever would have suspected at first glance. Now, how could he convince him? Did he really need to?

"Do you think I could have a friend of mine take a look at this? Maybe even… take it apart?"

"Take it apart?" Tom asked. A chain of thoughts whirled through his head. "That's a bit of a big ask. I don't have a lot here, and I could use a place to stay."

Sam slowly nodded. "I think that could be arranged…"

◇

After letting the phone charge, and finishing their meal, Tom and Sam headed back out on the road. They took the 75 back east and north through farm lands and past bits of nameless industrial buildings. They crossed the Maumee river over the Michael Disalle bridge. The grain elevator with its silos was still there on the north side, but the flashy casino to the south was notably absent. Tom still remembered when it was built. He was in college at the time and went there on his 21st birthday. It was younger than him, so of course it was nowhere to be seen.

They finally arrived at a small single story house in a quiet neighborhood just south of the University of Toledo on the other side of Dorr street. A large solitary oak tree stood at the edge of an otherwise unadorned lawn. It presented enough of a challenge to

Sam's semi truck that they parked on the other side of the street.

"Hey! Long time no see!" a portly man with glasses called from the modest porch of the little house.

"Hiya Bill! Indeed it has!" Sam called back.

"Oh, is that a passenger with you?"

"Uh, yes. This is Tom. Tom, this is Bill." After an exchange of handshakes, Sam continued, "Tom has something very interesting I know you're gonna wanna see."

"Oh?" Bill asked with a cocked eyebrow.

Sam nodded with an excited stare. "Oh yeah, definitely."

"Alright, well, uh, come in, come in!"

VII

"256 *Giga*bytes?" Bill asked incredulously.

"Yeah. It suits my needs. I don't take as many photos as some folks."

"You've gotta be shitting me! That's like… over two thousand floppies! Or —what?—a couple hundred hard drives at a thousand dollars a pop at least? How could you possibly fit that much storage in this thing?!"

"Solid state storage. No spinning platters or discs of any kind. If you doubt me, just look back through my photo library. How much storage do you think you'd need for images with this resolution or—?"

"Yeah, yeah. No need for the magic show again. I believe you, I do. This thing is insane! Like, out of this world." With that Bill gasped. "Maybe even literally…"

With that Bill peered at Tom for half a minute, then he looked to the phone and then back at Tom again. Tom coughed nervously and gave a half hearted smile.

"Okay," Bill continued looking over at Sam now. "What's the deal? Aliens? Is it aliens? Is this guy an alien?"

Tom burst out laughing, and Sam gave a nervous chuckle.

After regaining his composure, Tom tapped away on his phone and pulled up a system info screen. "I promise you I'm human, heh. This might explain it for you." With that he turned the phone towards Bill and pointed at the date/time stamp next to "Android security update."

"2023?"

Tom nodded in reply.

"Get outta town! I knew it!"

"Eh?" Tom asked in confusion.

"I told you time travel's possible!"

Sam rolled his eyes and sighed. "It doesn't make sense. Why aren't we encountering time travelers every minute of every day all the time? If time travel were possible in the not-too-distant fu-

ture, and there was so much future left
—"

"But that's just the point, Sam! There's not an infinite amount of future left. Long before even the eventual heat death of the universe the sun is going to go nova, and who knows how much time human civilization will last before then? And if it does, who knows how much we'll be exploring space? Perhaps traveling back in time on some alien world is more interesting than our own. And, even those folks who do time travel on Earth—what makes you think they'd want to come back to this time? What would make 1993 so interesting?"

"The web," Tom interjected. "Tomorrow CERN will release the software for the world wide web into the public domain."

"Aha! So that's it! See, Sam? It would have to be something notable."

"Well," Sam replied, "I have to admit it does seem slightly less outlandish than space aliens."

"It simply fits the facts. I mean with a device this advanced…" After Bill trailed off for a moment, he suddenly gasped and turned to Tom. "Is this it? Is this how you do it?"

"Do what?" Tom asked.

"Go back in time. Is this device your… time machine?"

"What?" Tom said and burst out laughing. "No, no no."

"Okay, so where is it? Are you hauling it in the back there?" Bill looked out the window towards Sam's truck across the street.

"I'm hauling light bulbs," Sam said with an eye roll.

"Look," Tom said with a sigh, "even in my time, time travel isn't a thing. At least as far as I know. How I got back here is… well, that's probably the most unbelievable part."

"Try me."

"Okay, well… last night I was out in the motel parking lot. I saw a shooting star and… I made a wish. I wished that tomorrow would be a day before the web. I went to sleep, and the next thing I knew I was here. Or I was now. This time. Whatever."

Bill paused and peered at Tom for a good half minute. Tom scratched the back of his neck and gave a little nervous cough. Finally Bill spoke up. "That's it? You wished upon a star? Like the goddamn Disney song?"

Uproarious laughter ensued, while Tom laughed along timidly, blushing with a bit of embarrassment. Sam slapped Tom on the back, then gripped his shoulder and gave him a little shake as he laughed. His necklace jangled softly amidst the laughter as he shook.

"Alright," Bill finally said, wiping a little tear from his eye. "So, I guess we'll chalk this one up to some kind of curious coincidence for now."

"Heh," Tom replied, "I'm just glad you guys don't think I'm completely crazy."

"Well if you are," Bill said, "you're in good company. I'm a little mad, myself." With that Bill gave a smirk and a wink, and Tom gave an awkward smile in return.

"In any case, I don't have much of anything now and… I could use a place to stay. If the phone is of interest to you—"

"Oh definitely! If you need a place to crash, feel free. I've got a guest room. Nothing fancy, but—"

"Oh thank you! I really appreciate this."

"Mi casa es su casa. In the mean time I have so many questions, man."

"Oh?"

"Yeah, do you guys have flying cars yet? And, like, how many channels on TV by then? Like a bazillion? Or was there a huge setback during Y2K? I mean, I'm guessing at least somebody survived and what not for you to come back."

"Uh… Why two what?"

"I'll let you guys get to it," Sam interjected with a chuckle. "In the mean time, I have to get back on the road and deliver these bulbs."

Jonathan Lee

VIII

FOR the rest of the day into the night, Tom walked Bill through the nuanced features of his phone and explained what he knew about its functions. It was fortunate that Tom had a background in IT, as Bill had a slew of technical inquiries. As it turned out Bill had a background in electrical engineering and was also a passionate part-time inventor, holding several patents and maintained a number of business connections with other entrepreneurial associates.

Bill denied wanting to take the phone apart—yet. It was too precious of an artifact and one about which he knew too little technically to risk destroying. In the mean time, Tom was sure he wanted to get back to his own time, and in that regard he had a most peculiar plan. His plan required research, and considering the vast unlimited resources of the web were not yet at his disposal, it would have to be conducted in a more old-fashioned way…

"You sure this is the right time and location?" Tom asked Bill in a near-whisper as they clicked and clacked along the tile floor of the entrance hall of the main library in downtown Toledo in the afternoon of the next day.

"Just because we don't have fancy look-up-everything portable terminals doesn't mean we don't know how to coordinate basic appointments, Tom. My friend goes to this club every week."

"Okay, okay."

They made their way to a side meeting room upstairs. Written on a big pad of white paper on a tripod outside the room were the words "Amateur Astronomer's Club."

Tom and Bill listened to the presentation and when the group opened it up to questions, Tom asked his question and received an answer. An exciting answer he was glad to hear. He only had to wait a week…

Wished Away

IX

OVER the course of the week, Sam happened to already have some time off. When he had mentioned that, Tom had re-marked "Ah, taking some time off for Star Wars Day, eh?" His question had been met with blank stares. (At that point in history "May the Fourth" was not as widely known for one reason or another.)

Sam came and visited Bill and his new friend Tom every day. The stories Tom shared of the future—even the relatively mundane ones—were immensely entertaining to both men. And the two men listened to Tom vent about his broken marriage and how his wife had left. They offered him what wisdom they had, and Tom took comfort from it as he listened. All in all, it was a bit of a bonding experience. And it was an hour or three Sam enjoyed spending away from his wife and kid—if only for a little while. (Sam's wife wasn't particularly thrilled at first, but he made up for it by watching his son earlier in the day while she went shopping.) It was finally Sam that had taken Tom back to the Simply 7 motel on the seventh night of May. Bill and

Sam had thrown Tom something of an informal farewell party, although both were quietly skeptical of Tom's plan.

Sam and Tom exited Sam's 1989 Chevy Suburban and walked out into the motel parking lot. There, staring out to the night sky, the foretold meteor shower started. At the sight of the first shooting star streaking across the heavens, Tom whispered the words he had planned: "I wish tomorrow was November 25th, 2023."

He had thought before to perhaps say his 30th birthday, but he physically felt much the same which meant perhaps it wouldn't work, since he was effectively 30 already. An exact date was probably safer.

"So… you really think this is going to work?"

"It's how I got here in the first place, as far as I know. It couldn't hurt, right?"

"I guess it couldn't."

They both stared up at the night sky for a quiet moment. A clear late spring night with a fair medley of stars shining out amidst their rural setting. It was less than ten minutes to midnight. If Tom was right, they would find out fairly soon.

"Well, if this works, we're gonna miss you," Sam finally said.

"Yeah, I'm gonna miss you guys too."

"But I totally get it, man. Family's important."

"Yeah…" Tom said wistfully and pulled out his pendant. He felt over its smooth surface, and looked over its design. He never knew what it had really meant to his father. A simple gold-plated circle bisected by a line segment. As he looked it over, lost in thought, Sam spoke up again.

"Where did you get *that?*"

"What? This pendant?"

"Yeah…" Sam said. And that's when he did something that made Tom's heart skip a beat and his jaw go slack. Sam pulled out his own pendant. Identical in every way. Even down to the tiny dent on one side.

"Wh-where did you get that?"

"I… made it."

"Wait—wait wait, Sam… you-you've never told me your family name."

"Wilson, why?"

"That's my family name too…"

"Really?"

"Wh-what's your full name?"

"Sebastian Samuel Wilson. But… only my wife calls me Sebastian."

"My mother. Sh-she only ever said his name was Sebastian."

"Tom?"

Tom frantically flipped through his phone's photos. And that's when he found it. An old photo he had forgotten about for some time. A scan of a photo originally taken in 1994. And that's when he realized why from the beginning Sam's face had looked familiar. For there he was holding little Thomas in his arms.

"Dad?" Tom asked with a lump in his throat as he showed his father the photo.

"Oh my god! Thomas!"

Sam grabbed his son and held him tightly, knowing the time was short. Possibly only a matter of minutes if Tom was right. Whatever doubts he might have had about his friend's fantastic story were in that moment gone. He had had a strange intuition about this stranger since the day they met. Like Tom, Sam felt something *familiar*. And now, as it turned out, that seemed to be quite literal.

Wiping away a tear Sam said with a crack in his voice, "Mary and I settled on Thomas just recently. That's what—what we were planning on naming Harry's little brother. Now that—that we know it's a boy. And now… now I think it's meant to be."

"If only I knew. There's so much I wanted to tell you."

"Heh, you've told me so much already. So much… son."

"Well there—there's one thing I'm not sure I ever got to tell you."

"What's that then, Tom?"

"I—I love you, Dad."

Sam snorted out a little laugh, sniffed away a tear, and thought back to that baby inside his wife's womb right now. The one that was due some time in November. Then he turned to the grown man standing before him, "I love you too, son."

After silently squeezing his father for a long minute or two, he let go and breathed out a sigh. He wiped away tears from his eyes like midnight dew. And when he opened his eyes… Sam was gone.

Wished Away

X

THE air was cold in the empty beat up parking lot. Even as the blur cleared from Tom's eyes, it was replaced with not so distant fog. The murky golden light. The tire shop with its ominous machinery. Even before he checked his phone, he knew what time it was. He looked anyways, down at a phone with full signal and checked the time. 12:00 AM. November 25th, 2023.

Never had success been so bitter.

But there was one silver lining to that cloudy night. When he looked at his pendant now, something in his mind unlocked. And for the first time in a long time, he could see his father's face clearly and remember his smile—weak as it was, lying there in the hospital bed. For a while, he wondered why he had left it to him and not his older brother. Could it be that back then he… knew?

Tom retired to his old motel room. He decided to actually undress this time. He tossed his clothes in the corner near his laptop bag and the waste basket filled with old Chinese food. He fell asleep staring at the red light of the little digital clock near his bed, hoping in his heart that when he awoke he might see something different there in its place.

◇

When he awoke, the digital clock was still there. And so was the old Chinese food. After he got dressed, cleaned out the trash, and packed up, he checked out of the motel. The less-than-social clerk at the counter of the little motel mumbled along a perfunctory conversation with a mixture of apathy and malaise, accepting his key card without issue.

"Kay, you're all set," the man muttered, and Tom nodded in return and walked out with a sigh.

Out in the parking lot, he unceremoniously summoned a ride in the ride sharing app on his phone. And then he checked his email while he waited for his ride to show up. He was back to the mundane wonders of the magical world that was the 21st century.

He pulled up to his mother's house in that quiet neighborhood in Perrysburg. The Christmas decorations were there—tacky reindeer and all. The lights, which would have sparkled in the night with quiet beauty, were just dull strings of unlit bulbs in the daytime. Light bulbs.

Why did he never know his father was once a semi-truck driver? Just a footnote in a life he never had known before. Should he be grateful now that he knew a little more? Now that he knew the man's smile and his laugh? Now that he had a taste of Sam's personality? A fleeting taste that was gone. He never knew before what he was missing. And now that he did, he missed it. He missed it so much.

Jonathan Lee

XI

"OH, Thomas, I'm so sorry," his mother said when she opened her lonely front door. "I heard what happened."

"You did…?" Tom asked, confused for a moment as she pulled him in for a hug.

"Yes, and it's just awful. I knew there were difficulties, but I just—I didn't see it coming."

Right. Amber. Somehow that all seemed so distant now.

"Come in, son, come in."

◆

Harry and his wife had already left Tom a present the night before. Tom had insisted he didn't want anything special for his birthday. Turning 30 was something he wasn't exactly thrilled about. For a few years now he had hoped to be a father by the time he was 30. So much for that.

"*Happy Birthday to you...*" his mother started to sing. In the empty little dining room where he was sitting, she brought out a cake with two little wax candles in the shape of a "3" and a "0." He tried to smile, but only managed to do so with the corners of his mouth. His eyes remained somber, betraying his sullen state. "Make a wish…" she stated after lighting the candles and finishing the song.

Her words sent a shiver down his spine. And he took her proposition unusually seriously for a lingering moment. He closed his eyes intently and thought to himself as was the tradition. If he said it outloud, it wouldn't come true, right? *I wish I could talk to him just one more time.*

He slowly opened his eyes and took a look around. He was still there in the dining room. And his mother was gazing at him with an ample dose of maternal concern. She gave him one of those sad close-mouthed smiles that comes with a head tilt and a sigh.

"I'm sure it'd be dumb of me to ask you if everything's all right."

"Heh," Tom replied. "I… I've actually been thinking about my father a bit lately. Why did you never tell me he went by Sam? Or that he was a truck driver for at least a year?"

"Oh, well… you never asked."

"Hm, I guess so," he said with a sigh.

"Y'know, that reminds me… I have a very peculiar gift that I've been holding on to for you for a long time."

"Oh?"

"Yes, for—well, heh—for 30 years now. I'll be right back."

Wished Away

Jonathan Lee

XII

SHE came back with a stack of notebooks. "Your father was very explicit that he wanted me to give you all this on your 30th birthday precisely. I would love to know what he wrote in here if you felt like sharing. But he also insisted it was for your eyes only, and he'd leave it up to you to share. All seemed a little silly, but then when he got sick… well, I've done my best to observe his wishes. Happy Birthday."

Tom took great care opening the first notebook. It was filled with letters. With teary awe-filled eyes, he poured over the first one…

Dear Thomas,

I rushed back to the Suburban to write this. When you disappeared, it was a bittersweet validation of the truth we both discovered this night. I wish I had more time with you. I know we both do. It's strange, because once I get home I know you'll be there. A much younger you, tucked away in your mother's womb.

Wished Away

I feel like I got the better end of the deal. Whatever this was, it gave me a glimpse into the future. And I must say I am so proud and grateful for the man you turned out to be.

I'm going to write you on a regular basis. I will make sure your mother gets them to you, but at a time when no one will think me insane. I don't know why you never got to know me before. I can't imagine ever leaving my sons. Did something happen to me?

Anyways, I'll keep writing. Letters to the future, I guess.

Your Father,
Sebastian S. Wilson

Tom flipped through the notebooks. There were dozens of entries. At least one for every month for three years. Some shorter, some longer. His eyes settled on one entry in particular: November 25th, 1993.

Dear Thomas,

You are so beautiful. When you were born, I cried at the sight of you. I remember you were a handsome man, but the memory is already fading. I wish I had had a fancy phone like yours. One where I could have taken as many pictures as I wished. As it was, there was only the one picture I have of you as an adult, thanks to Bill.

Wished Away

Tom stopped reading there and gasped. He had completely forgotten about that photo. And there it was, attached to the back of the page at the end of the letter. Bill and Sam with Tom in the middle, posing outside of the restaurant at the going away party. An old polaroid photograph taken by a stranger.

Finally, Tom flipped to the last entry. It was written a few days before his father died.

My Dear Thomas,

I know now why I didn't get to stay in your life. In a way, I'm glad it was this. People change over time, and for a long while I feared that some-

thing would have changed me into someone I couldn't recognize. I couldn't imagine ever leaving you by choice. And so I'm grateful, at least, that this choice wasn't mine.

Over the past few years, I've thought a lot about that night. Was there some guiding hand that brought us together as men for those few years? Some strange gift of grace that allowed me to see how things would turn out beyond my death? Whatever it was, I'm immensely grateful. I only hope you can move on—both from me, and the woman you once loved.

You can find love again, son.

One thing that came to my mind recently was how little was the time we had to say goodbye. But I've come to the conclusion that that too was a bit *of grace. A goodbye any longer than it was would have been just long enough for us to forget that 'goodbye' is what it truly was. How quickly we cease to recall how short is the time we have together.*

And so, considering how this letter might be my last, I'll try to end it short and sweet: Goodbye my dear son.

Love,
Dad

He poured over the notebooks, and they filled his heart with many things. Sometimes wisdom, sometimes laughter, and many times tears. Many things were contained in them which —even if they were shared in full— could not convey the depth of love contained in the heart of its writer, for a father's love knows no bounds. Neither height nor depth, nor even time.

Acknowledgments

I must thank first and foremost my wonderful wife who gave me two beautiful boys. "I cried at the sight" of their birth. The labor she endured—in all senses—to bring them into the world is something for which I'm immensely grateful.

To whatever extent I can be a good father, I have my mother to thank. Over the years, she has been the single greatest influence on my heart.

Lastly, my brother Jason who would guide me up mountains with "arms like a father" has always been a source of encouragement in this ongoing hobby of mine. Thanks, bro.

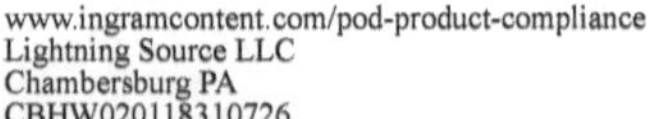